Picfic £9.99

D1101475

PET

NORTON'S HUT

To Isobelle, lover of mysteries.
J.M.

The illustrator wishes to acknowledge that this project has been assisted by the Commonwealth Government through the Australia Council, its arts funding and advisory body.

Thomas C. Lothian Pty Ltd
11 Munro Street, Port Melbourne, Victoria 3207

Text copyright © Jomden Pty Ltd 1998
Illustrations copyright © Peter Gouldthorpe 1998

First published 1998
Reprinted 1998

National Library of Australia
Cataloguing-in-Publication data:

Marsden, John, 1950-.
Norton's hut.

ISBN 0 85091 739 5.

1. Supernatural - Juvenile poetry.
2. Picture books for children.
3. Children's poetry, Australian.
I. Gouldthorpe, Peter. II. Title.

A821.3

Designed by David Salter
Colour separations by Chroma Graphics, Singapore
Printed in Hong Kong by Wing King Tong

NORTON'S HUT

John Marsden & Peter Gouldthorpe

Lothian
BOOKS

We caught our first glimpse of the hut late afternoon,
The sun kicking at our faces as we climbed.

But beyond the distant Governors, the clouds churned
like froth on water: we knew that in the valley
and across the plains a great boiling of weather
was taking place; the clouds a warning
of air about to pour across the peaks,
engulfing the mountain and us.

And so we quickened our pace and made towards the hut,
losing sight of it in the shadows of the spur,
but sure of our bearing, though our maps showed nothing
but a gully that twisted away down among the cliffs.

The air grew sharp and cold, the sun paled,
as we approached at last,
a single glass window catching the closing sparks of day.

Our noisy confidence brought us to the door
but there our voices stilled
at a movement from within and a stammer of white smoke
from the chimney. Someone here before us!

We knocked and opened, a little awkwardly,
lifting the door to clear the step,
disconcerted by the dark inside.

A man sat by the fire, hands stretched to the poor warmth
of the young flames; the fire new-laid
and struggling into life.

He barely nodded his response
as we filled the hut with noise,
fetching wood and spreading packs and clothes
across the room.

Outside, mist, cold and cloud flooded over the peak
and the wind pushed and pulled and groaned
around the hut. Only our voices
and the fitful fire kept us warm.

The man, his white face young and nervous, said nothing
while the wind grew to gale,
but at each terror of gust he glanced up
and trembled, and huddled closer to the comfort
that the flames alone could give.

Snow stung at the door; not the soft snow of dreams
but the bitter snow that bites at the skin
and darts like death in the wild air.

We ate early; the man at the fire refused our food,
though having none himself.

Subdued by his silence, we huddled into sleeping bags
while he wrapped himself in an old blanket. Through the
long night we lay half-awake,
feeling the hut shiver in the storm,
and listening to the timber cry in the tossing wind.

In the morning the man had gone, but we,
still deep in snow and torn at

every time we stepped outside,
stayed three days trapped in the hut,

until at last we awoke to the peace of blue
and the calm of white,
the air still as music and the mountains settled

into a spreading dawn that reached
from Solitude in the north
to the Bluff in the south.

We left at eight,
picking our way along the Razorback,
making for Tribulation and Clinker,
moving quickly, after days of static time,
three days when time had ceased
to move.

From Wallambi's peak we looked back,
searching for the hut,
but unable to pick out its brown frame against
the throat of the dark gully. It seemed to have
faded back into the cold mountains,
lost in the remote world of the Great Divide,
beyond the reach of those who travel
the slight tracks of the high ridges.

We camped that night by Clinker's cold lake,
the white bones of dead trees stiff in the water,
and told the tale of the storm around a campfire
to men who know the mountains passively,
without emotion, as sailors the ocean.
They stared at us blankly.
'That was Norton's hut, burnt down in '56,
young Norton still inside. They say he built his fire big
for warmth, the blizzard blowing snow against the walls
and howling at his door. Nothing there now but rocks'.

They gazed into the coals.

On the lake a breeze stirred the water
and sent ripples brushing towards the dead trees.

Norton's Hut

We caught our first glimpse of the hut late afternoon,
The sun kicking at our faces as we climbed.

But beyond the distant Governors, the clouds churned
like froth on water: we knew that in the valley
and across the plains a great boiling of weather
was taking place; the clouds a warning
of air about to pour across the peaks,
engulfing the mountain and us.

And so we quickened our pace and made towards the hut,
losing sight of it in the shadows of the spur,
but sure of our bearing, though our maps showed nothing
but a gully that twisted away down among the cliffs.

The air grew sharp and cold, the sun paled,
as we approached at last,
a single glass window catching the closing sparks of day.

Our noisy confidence brought us to the door
but there our voices stilled
at a movement from within and a stammer of white smoke
from the chimney. Someone here before us!

We knocked and opened, a little awkwardly,
lifting the door to clear the step,
disconcerted by the dark inside.

A man sat by the fire, hands stretched to the poor warmth
of the young flames; the fire new-laid
and struggling into life.

He barely nodded his response
as we filled the hut with noise,

fetching wood and spreading packs and clothes
across the room.

Outside, mist, cold and cloud flooded over the peak
and the wind pushed and pulled and groaned
around the hut. Only our voices
and the fitful fire kept us warm.

The man, his white face young and nervous, said nothing
while the wind grew to gale,
but at each terror of gust he glanced up
and trembled, and huddled closer to the comfort
that the flames alone could give.

Snow stung at the door; not the soft snow of dreams
but the bitter snow that bites at the skin
and darts like death in the wild air.

We ate early; the man at the fire refused our food,
though having none himself.

Subdued by his silence, we huddled into sleeping bags
while he wrapped himself in an old blanket.

Through the long night we lay half-awake,
feeling the hut shiver in the storm,
and listening to the timber cry in the tossing wind.

In the morning the man had gone, but we,
still deep in snow and torn at
every time we stepped outside,
stayed three days trapped in the hut,
until at last we awoke to the peace of blue
and the calm of white,
the air still as music and the mountains settled
into a spreading dawn that reached
from Solitude in the north
to the Bluff in the south.

We left at eight,
picking our way along the Razorback,
making for Tribulation and Clinker,
moving quickly, after days of static time,
three days when time had ceased
to move.

From Wallambi's peak we looked back,
searching for the hut.
but unable to pick out its brown frame against
the throat of the dark gully. It seemed to have
faded back into the cold mountains,
lost in the remote world of the Great Divide,
beyond the reach of those who travel
the slight tracks of the high ridges.

We camped that night by Clinker's cold lake,
the white bones of dead trees stiff in the water,
and told the tale of the storm around a campfire
to men who know the mountains passively,
without emotion, as sailors the ocean.
They stared at us blankly.

'That was Norton's hut, burnt down in '56,
young Norton still inside. They say he built his fire big
for warmth, the blizzard blowing snow against the walls
and howling at his door. Nothing there now
but rocks'.

They gazed into the coals.

On the lake a breeze stirred the water
and sent ripples brushing towards the dead trees.